The
AIRPLANE

Richard and Louise Spilsbury

Heinemann Library

Chicago, Illinois

www.heinemannraintree.com
Visit our website to find out
more information about
Heinemann-Raintree books.

To order:

☎ Phone 888-454-2279

🖳 Visit www.heinemannraintree.com
to browse our catalog and order online.

© 2011 Heinemann Library
an imprint of Capstone Global Library, LLC
Chicago, Illinois

All rights reserved. No part of this publication may be
reproduced or transmitted in any form or by any means,
electronic or mechanical, including photocopying,
recording, taping, or any information storage and
retrieval system, without permission in writing from
the publisher.

Edited by Louise Galpine and Laura Knowles
Designed by Philippa Jenkins
Original illustrations © Capstone Global Library Ltd 2011
Illustrated by KJA-artists.com
Picture research by Mica Brancic

Originated by Capstone Global Library Ltd
Printed and bound in China by CTPS

15 14 13 12 11
10 9 8 7 6 5 4 3 2 1

Library of Congress Cataloging-in-Publication Data
Spilsbury, Richard, 1963-
   The airplane / Richard and Louise Spilsbury.
      p. cm. -- (Tales of invention)
   Includes bibliographical references and index.
   ISBN 978-1-4329-3830-7 (hc) -- ISBN 978-1-4329-
3837-6 (pb) 1. Airplanes--History--Juvenile literature.
2. Aeronautics--History--Juvenile literature. I. Spilsbury,
Louise. II. Title.
   TL547.S7177 2011
   629.133'34--dc22

                                          2009049149

Acknowledgments
The author and publisher are grateful to the following
for permission to reproduce copyright material:: Alamy
Images pp. 11 (© INTERFOTO), 14 (© Marka), 25
bottom (© George Impey); Corbis pp. 9 (© Reuters),
18 (© Hulton-Deutsch Collection), 19 (Bettmann), 26
(epa/© Hyungwon Kang); Getty Images pp. 8 (Science
& Society Picture Library), 12 (Time Life Pictures/
Mansell), 13 (Science & Society Picture Library), 20
(Time Life Pictures/J. R. Eyerman), 24 (U.S. Navy/John
Gay), 27 (AFP Photo/Aero-News Network/Jim Campbell);
Jon Linney p. 7 (http://firstflight.open.ac.uk);
Photolibrary pp. 4 (Science Photo Library), 15, 16 (Tips
Italia/Antique Research Center), 17 (Imagestate/Art
Media), 21 (De Agostini Editore/DEA Picture Library),
23 (Hemis/Alain Felix); TopFoto p. 10 (The Granger
Collection, New York).

Cover photographs of an airbus 380 reproduced with
permission of Reuters/© Benoit Tessier and a Wright
biplane at the Helena, Montana, State Fair reproduced
with permission of Getty/Hulton Archive.

We would like to thank Ian Graham for his invaluable
help in the preparation of this book.

Every effort has been made to contact copyright holders
of material reproduced in this book. Any omissions will
be rectified in subsequent printings if notice is given to
the publisher.

Disclaimer
All the Internet addresses (URLs) given in this book
were valid at the time of going to press. However, due
to the dynamic nature of the Internet, some addresses
may have changed, or sites may have changed or
ceased to exist since publication. While the author
and publisher regret any inconvenience this may cause
readers, no responsibility for any such changes can be
accepted by either the author or the publisher.

CONTENTS

Look for these boxes •⟶

R0431053527

BEFORE AIRPLANES 4

THE FIRST FLYING MACHINES ... 6

THE FIRST AIRPLANES 12

AIRPLANES TAKE OFF 18

JET PLANES 22

INTO THE FUTURE 26

TIMELINE 28

GLOSSARY 30

FIND OUT MORE 31

INDEX 32

Biographies

These boxes tell you about the life of inventors, the dates when they lived, and their important discoveries.

Setbacks

Here we tell you about the experiments that didn't work, the failures, and the accidents.

EUREKA!

These boxes tell you about important events and discoveries, and what inspired them.

Any words appearing in the text in bold, **like this**, are explained in the glossary.

TIMELINE

BEFORE AIRPLANES

Today, many people fly in airplanes when they go on vacation or on business trips. Most of the world's armies have airplanes for fighting. People probably started to dream about flying hundreds of thousands of years ago, when they saw birds gliding through the air.

In 1783 two French inventors, the Montgolfier brothers, made the first machine to carry people up into the air. Hot air rises, so when they filled a giant fabric balloon with hot air, it lifted into the sky. This was a lot of fun, but it was not the same as flying like a bird.

This early hot air balloon was launched in front of crowds in Lyon, France, on New Year's Day, 1784.

EUREKA!

A duck, a chicken, and a sheep became the first living creatures to fly in a Montgolfier hot air balloon during a trial run in France on September 19, 1783.

around 1000 BCE—The kite is invented in China

Lifting up

Making a machine that can fly like a bird is difficult because of the different **forces** acting on it. A force is a push or a pull.

Gravity is a force that pulls everything down toward Earth. **Lift** pulls things upward. For an airplane to get up into the sky, the lift force must be greater than the gravity force.

Thrust is a force that moves things forward. **Drag** pushes against things that are moving and slows them down or pushes them backward. For an airplane to move forward when it is in the sky, the thrust must be greater than the drag.

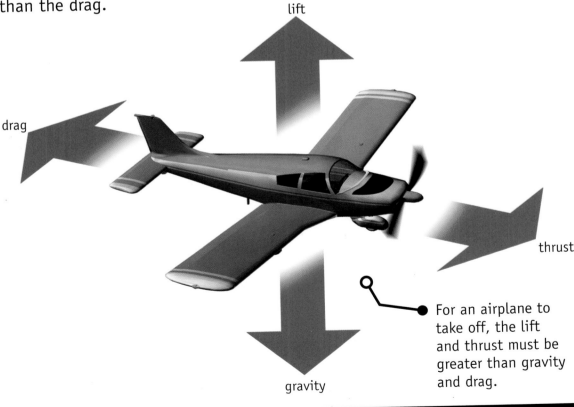

lift

drag

thrust

gravity

For an airplane to take off, the lift and thrust must be greater than gravity and drag.

around 1500 ce—Artist Leonardo da Vinci draws designs for flying machines

1783—First flight in a hot air balloon

THE FIRST FLYING MACHINES

In 1809 English scientist George Cayley became the first person to explain how the curved shape of a bird's wing helps to create **lift**.

Wing shape and lift

When a wing moves through the air, it cuts the airflow in half. Some air travels above the wing, and some air travels below it. The air going over the top of a curved wing has to go faster to keep up with the air flowing below the wing, because it has further to go. When air moves faster, it has less pushing power. When air on top of the wing is pushing less strongly than the air below, the wing is pushed upward.

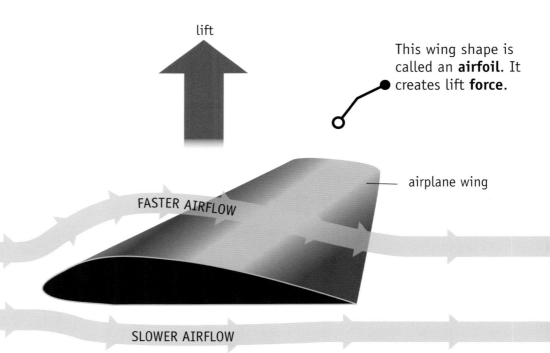

lift

This wing shape is called an **airfoil**. It creates lift **force**.

airplane wing

FASTER AIRFLOW

SLOWER AIRFLOW

Cayley's glider, the *New Flyer*, had wings made of long sticks with fabric stretched over them.

The first glider

In 1853 George Cayley used his discoveries about the shape of birds' wings to make the world's first **glider** that could carry a fully grown person. A glider is a light aircraft that flies without an engine. To get the glider into the air, it was pulled down a slope so its wings were angled downward. As the glider raced downhill, air was forced under the wings, creating more and more lift until the glider was able to take off.

7

George Cayley *(1773–1854)*

George Cayley was born in Yorkshire, England. As a child he was fascinated by flight, and when he grew up he became a scientist. He made many sketches and models of flying machines, including a 1.5-meter- (5-foot-) long model **glider** in 1804. At that time, most inventors thought aircraft would need flapping wings to fly. By watching seagulls, Cayley realized that wings of the right shape could get enough **lift** to glide.

Cayley invented many things apart from gliders. He invented a telescope as well as "caterpillar" tracks for vehicles like tractors. After seeing one of the first rail crashes in Great Britain, he also invented a cowcatcher. This was a metal frame at the front of a train that cleared the track ahead of it.

This modern copy of Cayley's *New Flyer* helps to show what it would have been like to fly in an early glider. In this photograph, the glider has only lifted a little way off the ground.

Landing problems

Cayley was too old to fly his own glider in 1853, so he told his driver to do it. To make the glider take off, a team of men used ropes to pull it down a steep slope. The airplane glided for some distance, but then crashed. When the driver climbed out of the wreckage, he quit his job, saying to Cayley: "Please, Sir George, I wish to give notice [that I am quitting]. I was hired to drive and not to fly."

Better gliders

German engineers Otto and Gustav Lilienthal continued Cayley's work. They experimented with **gliders** that had flapping wings and others with two wings. Otto did most of the flying, and he learned to bend and turn the wings to control the direction that the gliders flew in.

Otto and Gustav Lilienthal
(1848–1896 and 1849–1933)

When Otto Lilienthal (left) and his brother Gustav were young, they experimented with wings by sewing real bird feathers together. When they grew up, they built a hill on open land so that Otto could fly their gliders off it in all directions. Otto made more than 2,000 successful flights, before dying after a glider accident in 1896. After Otto's death, Gustav worked on wing-flapping aircraft, but he never managed to make them fly.

 Here, Otto Lilienthal is making a test flight, watched by a crowd near Berlin, Germany, in 1892.

The next step

A glider can only stay in the air for a short time because **drag** slows it down until it stops and has to land. For an aircraft to fly forward, it needs a strong **thrust force** to beat drag. In 1874 French navy officer Félix du Temple built an aircraft with a **steam engine**. Ten years later, Russian inventor Aleksandr Mozhaysky built a similar aircraft. The engines made steam that turned **propellers** to push the machines through the air. However, both aircrafts were too heavy, and neither managed to fly properly!

 Setbacks

After rolling down a long ramp, Mozhaysky's heavy machine hopped for a short distance, then hit the ground and broke its wings. Mozhaysky was uninjured. He gave up trying to fly but continued to research air propellers.

11

1853—Cayley invents a glider that can carry a fully grown person

THE FIRST AIRPLANES

The first real airplane took to the air in 1903. The *Wright Flyer*, built by the U.S. Wright brothers, flew for only 12 seconds, but the invention changed the world. The Wright brothers had made the first powered flying machine that could take off and be fully controlled in the air.

The *Wright Flyer*

The *Wright Flyer* was a light wooden **biplane** with two fabric wings on each side. Car engines were too heavy to use, so their mechanic, Charlie Taylor, helped them to build their own gasoline engine made of aluminium, which is a strong but light metal.

This photograph shows the first flight of the *Wright Flyer* in 1903.

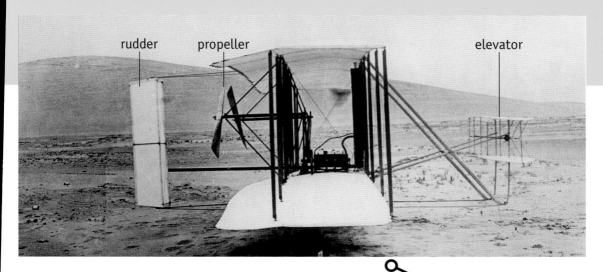

rudder   propeller   elevator

How it worked

This photograph of the *Wright Flyer* shows its propeller, rudder, and elevators.

The engine on the *Wright Flyer* turned two **propellers**. Propellers have metal blades shaped like **airfoils**. When they spin, they pull the airplane forward just like its wings lift it upward.

To control the airplane, Orville pulled cables attached to the wings and **rudder.** By twisting the wings and turning the rudder slightly one way or the other, the airplane rolled right or left. By using a lever to tilt flaps at the front of the plane, called elevators, the airplane moved up or down.

Setbacks

Wilbur completed two longer flights than Orville had made, but on his third flight, the plane became damaged. As the brothers were carrying it back to be repaired, a strong wind blew the airplane over and destroyed it.

EUREKA!

On Orville's first flight he flew for 37 meters (120 feet) before landing safely. Although this was not a long distance, it was a huge achievement.

13

1874—French navy officer Félix du Temple tries to make an aircraft with a **steam engine**

14

1884—Russian inventor Aleksandr Mozhaysky attempts flight in a steam-powered aircraft

Wilbur and Orville Wright *(1867–1912 and 1871–1948)*

The Wright brothers' interest in flying began in 1878, when their father came back from a business trip with a gift of a rubber band-powered helicopter. The boys immediately began to make copies of it. Their interest continued as they grew up and ran a printing business from 1890 and a bicycle shop from 1892.

They studied the work of other aircraft inventors and did experiments with kites and **gliders**. From 1900 to 1903, they made and flew a number of gliders to discover how a plane could be controlled. After 1903 they made and tested many more planes, and by 1905 the latest *Wright Flyer* could turn figure-eight shapes in the sky.

The Wright brothers tried to sell their invention to governments around the world, but at first people thought they were crazy. Finally, in 1908 they started to make and sell airplanes for buyers such as the U.S. Army. They went on improving their airplanes and displaying them to crowds of people. In New York in 1909, one million amazed spectators watched Wilbur fly. The brothers became celebrities.

A bat-winged plane

After the Wright brothers' success became known, French inventor Clément Ader claimed he had made the first powered flight. He said he had flown on October 9, 1890, in a steam-powered, bat-winged **monoplane**, which he named the *Éole* (pronounced "ee-ol"). There was never any proof that Ader had flown.

This photograph shows Clement Ader's aircraft, the *Éole*.

15

Going further

In 1908 the *Daily Mail* newspaper in the United Kingdom offered a prize of £1,000 (about $150,000 in today's money) to the first person to fly across the English Channel. On July 25, 1909, French inventor Louis Blériot's **monoplane**, the *Blériot XI*, made the crossing in just 36 minutes. Blériot's engine was less powerful than a modern scooter's, but it carried his wood-and-cloth plane safely across the 35-kilometer (22-mile) stretch of water. After his famous flight, Blériot started an airplane business, building more than 800 aircraft by 1914.

Setbacks

Many people thought French pilot Hubert Latham would be the first to cross the Channel, but on two attempts the engine of his plane stopped working and he crashed into the sea.

Here the *Blériot XI* can be seen making the first flight across the English Channel.

1903—The Wright brothers make the first powered flight in the *Wright Flyer*

1905—The new, improved *Wright Flyer* can be fully controlled in the sky

1908—The Wright brothers start to make and sell airplanes

1908—Alfred Wilm creates duralumin, a new metal for making airplane parts

1900

1910

World War I airplanes

During World War I (1914–18), airplanes became weapons of war. At first, armies only used planes to spot where enemy troops were on the ground. Some pilots began to take guns up with them to fire at targets. This led to the invention of new fighter planes. These planes had machine guns attached to the front to shoot down enemy aircraft.

EUREKA!

In 1908 German inventor Alfred Wilm created a new metal. Duralumin was a mix of aluminium and other metals, and it was very strong but very light. The Germans kept the discovery a secret during World War I, when they used it to make German fighter planes.

This British bomber plane has been shot down in France in 1917.

17

1909—Louis Blériot's monoplane, the *Blériot XI*, makes the first crossing of the English Channel

AIRPLANES TAKE OFF

During the first part of the 1900s, airplanes flew higher and further than before and the first passenger planes were built. The Douglas DC3, invented in 1935 by American Arthur Raymond, was the first airplane to carry enough passengers to make a profit. Engine noise inside was reduced by having thick carpet on the cabin floor and rubber around the engines.

The Douglas DC3 made flying comfortable and quieter for the 24 passengers it carried.

More people wanted to fly after reading about the record-breaking flights of pilots such as Charles Lindbergh and Amelia Earhart. Lindbergh made the first **transatlantic** solo flight in 1927, and Earhart became the first woman to fly across the Atlantic alone in 1932.

1927—Charles Lindbergh's first transatlantic solo flight

1928—World's first air ambulance service starts up

In many of the first air ambulances, patients were strapped to the airplane in their stretchers.

Air ambulances

Doctors had long realized that airplanes could carry people to the hospital in emergencies, such as during wars. The first successful **air ambulance** service, called the Flying Doctor service, was set up in 1928 in Australia, where many people lived far from a hospital. Most air ambulances today are helicopters, because these can take off and land **vertically** in places planes cannot go, such as rooftops. The large blades above a helicopter's body are shaped like **airfoils**. When they spin, they create **lift** and the helicopter takes off.

EUREKA!

The first truly successful helicopter was the VS-300, built by Russian-American engineer Igor Sikorsky in 1939. The small blades at the back of the helicopter turn in the opposite direction of the big blades, to prevent the helicopter body from spinning around.

19

1932—Amelia Earhart is the first woman to fly across the Atlantic Ocean alone

1935—Flying boat *China Clipper* makes the first flight across the Pacific Ocean

1935—**Radar** is invented

1939—World's first successful helicopter is invented

1939—First turbojet-powered airplane flight

1940

Flying boats

In the 1930s and 1940s, wealthy passengers traveled in flying boats. These were airplanes designed to land on and take off from water. The planes had boat-shaped bottoms or **floats** on the wings, so that they would not sink. A flying boat named the *China Clipper* made the first flight across the Pacific Ocean in 1935. Some flying boats were huge, with bedrooms, dining rooms, and lounges!

Howard Hughes
(1905–1976)

American Howard Hughes was a multimillionaire and plane fanatic who set many airplane speed records. In November 1947 he built the giant, eight-engine H-4 Hercules flying boat. With its wingspan of 98 meters (320 feet), it was designed to carry 750 passengers. Hughes flew it once for a short distance, but it was too heavy to fly properly.

Howard Hughes' H-4 Hercules is landing on water after its first and only flight.

1940–41—Germany uses airplanes to drop bombs over the United Kingdom

1947—Chuck Yeager breaks the sound barrier in the world's first **supersonic** flight

1947—Howard Hughes builds the giant, eight-engine H-4 Hercules flying boat

1940

1950

World War II planes

Airplanes played a very important role in
World War II (1939–45). Bombers were big planes with
several engines and large **fuel** tanks, so they could
travel long distances to drop bombs. Fighters were
made of light aluminium metal so they could be quick
and move easily in sky fights against enemy planes.

British fighter pilots were guided toward their targets
by new **radar** systems. Radar was invented in 1935 by
Scottish scientist Robert Alexander Watson-Watt. By
sending **radio waves** into the sky and studying the
echoes that bounced back when those radio waves
hit an object, command centers could locate enemy
aircraft and tell pilots their position by radio.

Attacks by
German bombers
on Britain in
1940 were known
as the Blitz.

21

JET PLANES

The invention of the turbojet engine greatly increased the distance and speed that airplanes could travel.

How turbojet engines work

A turbojet engine sucks air into the front part of the engine. A **compressor** squeezes the air into a **combustion chamber**, where **fuel** is added and burned to create hot gases. Some of these gases turn a **turbine**, which works the compressor. The rest are blasted out of a nozzle, creating the **thrust force** needed to push the airplane forward.

This diagram shows how a turbojet engine works.

Setbacks

British engineer Frank Whittle designed the first turbojet engine in 1930, but he had problems getting the engine to work properly, and it took years to develop. The world's first turbojet-powered flight was the German Heinkel He 178 in 1939, using an engine built by German engineer Hans von Ohain.

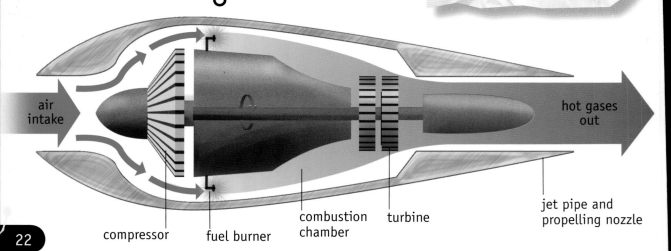

air intake

hot gases out

compressor   fuel burner   combustion chamber   turbine   jet pipe and propelling nozzle

direction of airplane

Jet airliners

Airliners are jet planes that carry passengers. The first jet airliner was the de Havilland Comet in 1949. It could fly at 800 kilometers (500 miles) per hour and carry 36 people. Bigger and faster jet planes were built as more people wanted to travel abroad for vacations. **Jumbo jets** are giant airliners that can carry huge numbers of passengers. The first jumbo jet, the Boeing 747, flew its first passenger service in 1970, and it could carry about 350 people.

EUREKA!

In 2005 a new double-decker superjumbo jet with seating for about 500 people took its first flight. Airbus A380 is so big that there would be room to park 70 cars on its wings!

The Airbus A380 is the world's largest passenger plane.

23

1976—Concorde is the first **supersonic** jet to operate a passenger service

1980

Breaking the sound barrier

In 1947 U.S. pilot Chuck Yeager became the first person to fly at **supersonic** speeds. At the height that airplanes fly, sound travels at about 1,100 kilometers (700 miles) per hour. When a plane goes almost as fast as sound, it catches up with the **sound waves** traveling in front of it. It compresses, or squeezes, them together into a barrier just in front of itself. When a jet breaks through this sound barrier, the compressed air spreads out suddenly. When this shock wave hits the ground, people hear a sonic boom—a noise like a giant clap of thunder.

EUREKA!

In 1976 Concorde became the first supersonic jet to operate a passenger service. It could fly at Mach 2—twice the speed of sound.

This is the moment a supersonic jet breaks through the sound barrier.

1989—First test flights of stealth bomber airplanes

This is a
U.S. Air Force
stealth bomber.

Jet fighters

Over time, armies have developed different kinds of jet fighter planes. Harrier jump jets were invented in the 1960s by British engineer Sydney Camm. Harriers can jump straight up into the air when side engines are aimed downward to thrust the jet up. Stealth bombers were developed in the 1980s. These planes are shaped to reduce **radar** reflections and made of materials such as radar-absorbing paint. This lets them sneak up on targets without being spotted by enemy radar systems.

Sydney Camm
(1893–1966)

Sydney Camm trained to be a carpenter but was fascinated by model planes. He became an airplane designer in 1923. He designed many planes, including the famous Hawker Hurricane fighting planes of World War II, but the Harrier jump jet was his last.

Harrier jump jets can take off **vertically**!

INTO THE FUTURE

Today, buying an airplane ticket is cheaper than ever before, and there are a huge number of planes traveling across our skies. This is not good news for everyone. Some people are protesting about new runways being built on areas of countryside, and others worry that airplanes use too much **fuel** at a time when oil is running out, and that burning fuel causes air **pollution**.

New designs

In the future, more planes may be made of lighter materials such as carbon fiber, which would use less fuel. New designs will create more **lift** once planes are moving through the air. Future planes may also be powered with **renewable** sources of energy, such as solar power, rather than oil.

Solar cells on this plane Helios, which first flew on solar power in 2001, convert the energy in sunlight into electricity to make it fly.

2003—First flight of Helios, a solar-powered airplane

2004—SpaceShipOne is the world's first private airplane to fly to the edge of space

2005—The world's first superjumbo, Airbus A380, takes to the air

Space planes

In the future, passenger planes may also fly to new destinations, such as the Moon! Early spaceships were transported into space by rockets, which could only be used once. In 1981 a space shuttle was launched into space like a rocket but it landed back on Earth like a plane, ready to be used again. Some engineers think that future space planes may be run by high-powered jet engines.

Could ordinary people be taking flights into space in the future, on airplanes like SpaceShipOne?

EUREKA!

In 2004 U.S. businessman Burt Rutan's SpaceShipOne became the first private airplane to fly 100 kilometers (60 miles) above Earth to the edge of space.

27

TIMELINE

around 1000 BCE
The kite is invented in China

around 1500 CE
Artist Leonardo da Vinci draws designs for flying machines

1783
First flight in a hot air balloon

1804
George Caley builds a 1.5-m- (5-ft.-) long model **glider**

1908
The Wright brothers start to make and sell airplanes

1905
The new and improved *Wright Flyer* can be fully controlled in the sky

1903
The Wright brothers make the first powered flight in the *Wright Flyer*

1908
German inventor Alfred Wilm creates duralumin, a new metal for making airplane parts

1909
Louis Blériot's **monoplane**, the *Blériot XI*, makes the first crossing of the English Channel

1927
Charles Lindbergh's first **transatlantic** solo flight

1966
Harrier jump jets are developed

1947
Howard Hughes builds the giant, eight-engine H-4 Hercules flying boat

1947
Chuck Yeager breaks the sound barrier in the world's first **supersonic** flight

1970
The first **jumbo jet**, the Boeing 747, enters passenger service

1976
Concorde is the first supersonic jet to operate a passenger service

1989
First test flights of stealth bomber airplanes

1809
Cayley publishes a book explaining important facts about flight, such as how wing shape creates **lift**

1849
First successful glider flight carrying a person, the 10-year-old son of one of Caley's servants

1853
Cayley invents a glider that can carry a fully grown person

1891
German engineer Otto Lilienthal is the first person to make safe, repeated gliding flights

1884
Russian inventor Aleksandr Mozhaysky attempts flight in a steam-powered aircraft

1874
French navy officer Félix du Temple tries to make an aircraft with a **steam engine**

1928
World's first **air ambulance** service starts up

1932
Amelia Earhart is the first woman to fly across the Atlantic Ocean alone

1935
Flying boat *China Clipper* makes the first flight across the Pacific Ocean

1935
Radar is invented

1940–1941
Germany uses airplanes to drop bombs over Great Britain. This is known as the Blitz.

1939
First turbojet-powered airplane flight

1939
World's first successful helicopter is invented

2003
First flight of Helios, a solar-powered airplane

2004
SpaceShipOne is the world's first private airplane to fly to the edge of space

2005
The world's first superjumbo, Airbus A380, takes to the air

GLOSSARY

air ambulance special aircraft that carries patients to the hospital

airfoil curved part of an airplane's wing that helps it fly

airliner large plane that carries passengers

biplane airplane with two sets of wings, one above the other

combustion chamber part of an engine in which fuel is burned

compressor machine that compresses (squeezes) air or other gases

drag force of air that pushes against objects

floats light objects that float in water

force push or pull that makes things move in a particular way

fuel material that produces heat or power

glider light aircraft that flies without an engine

gravity force that attracts objects in space together. Gravity pulls things toward the center of Earth.

internal combustion engine engine that produces power by burning fuel inside it

jumbo jet large airplane that can carry several hundred passengers

lift upward push of air on an aircraft as it flies. Lift is a kind of force.

monoplane aircraft with one set of wings

pollution something that makes air, soil, or water dirty

propeller device with two or more metal blades that turn quickly

radar method of spotting distant objects using radio waves

radio waves form of energy that moves through the air

renewable something that will not run out. Renewable energy is energy generated from natural resources, such as sunlight, wind, and waves.

rudder flat blade that sticks up at the back of a plane and turns the plane left and right

solar cell device that changes energy from sunlight into electricity

sound wave vibration in the air caused by sound

steam engine engine that produces steam to move parts, usually by burning fuel

supersonic faster than the speed of sound

thrust force produced by an engine to push a plane forward

transatlantic across the Atlantic Ocean

turbine machine with a set of blades that spin when driven by steam, gas, water, or wind

vertically straight up or down

FIND OUT MORE

Books

Hofer, Charles. *World's Fastest Machines: Airplanes*. New York: PowerKids, 2008.

Platt, Richard. *Experience Flight*. New York: Dorling Kindersley, 2006.

Stone, Tanya Lee. *Amelia Earhart*. New York: Dorling Kindersley, 2007.

Websites

To find out more about the Wright brothers, go to:
www.wright-brothers.org

Find out more about the history of flight at:
www.ueet.nasa.gov/StudentSite/historyofflight.html

Learn about aerodynamics at:
www.ueet.nasa.gov/StudentSite/dynamicsofflight.html

Places to visit

Smithsonian National Air and Space Museum
Independence Ave at 6th Street, SW
Washington, D.C. 20560
www.nasm.si.edu

The Museum of Flight
9404 East Marginal Way S.
Seattle, Washington 98108-4097
www.museumofflight.org

AirVenture Museum
P.O. Box 3086
Oshkosh, Wisconsin 54903-3086
www.airventuremuseum.org

INDEX

Ader, Clément 15
air ambulances 19
Airbus A380 23
airflow 6
airfoils 6, 13, 19
airliners 23

biplanes 12
Blériot, Louis 16
Blitz 21
Boeing 747 23
bombers 17, 21

Camm, Sydney 25
carbon fiber 26
caterpillar tracks 9
Cayley, George 6, 7–9
China Clipper 20
combustion chambers 22
compressors 22
Concorde 24

De Havilland Comet 23
Douglas DC3 18
drag 5, 11
duralumin 17

Earhart, Amelia 18
elevators 13
engines 6, 11, 12, 16, 18,
    21, 22, 25, 27
Éole 15

fighter planes 17, 21, 25
first airplanes 12–17
floats 20
flying boats 20
forces 5, 11, 22
fuel 6, 22, 26

gliders 7, 9–11, 15
gravity 5

H-4 Hercules 20
Harrier jump jets 25
Hawker Hurricane 25
Heinkel He 178 22
helicopters 19
Helios 26
hot air balloons 4
Hughes, Howard 20

internal combustion
    engines 6

jet planes 22–25
jumbo jets 23

kites 4

Latham, Hubert 16
Leonardo da Vinci 5
lift 5, 6, 7, 9, 19, 26
Lilienthal, Otto and Gustav
    10, 11
Lindbergh, Charles 18

monoplanes 16
Montgolfier brothers 4
Mozhaysky, Aleksandr 11

New Flyer 7, 9

Ohain, Hans von 22

pollution 26
propellers 11, 13

radar 21, 25
radio waves 21
Raymond, Arthur 18
renewable energy 26
Rutan, Burt 27

Sikorsky, Igor 19
solar-powered planes 26
sonic boom 24
sound barrier 24
sound waves 24
space planes 27
space shuttles 27
SpaceShipOne 27
stealth bombers 25
steam engines 11
superjumbo jets 23
supersonic flight 24

Temple, Félix du 11
thrust 5, 11, 22
transatlantic flights 18
turbines 22
turbojet engines 22

vertical takeoff 19, 25
VS-300 19

Watson-Watt, Alexander 21
Whittle, Frank 22
Wilm, Alfred 17
World War I 17
World War II 21, 25
Wright, Orville and Wilbur
    12–15
Wright Flyer 12–13, 15

Yeager, Chuck 24